# MY PERFECT COUSIN

# MY PERFECT COUSIN

**KAREN McCOMBIE**

ILLUSTRATED BY
SOFIA MILLER SALAZAR

Barrington Stoke

Published by Barrington Stoke
An imprint of HarperCollins*Publishers*
1 Robroyston Gate, Glasgow, G33 1JN

www.barringtonstoke.co.uk

HarperCollins*Publishers*
Macken House, 39/40 Mayor Street Upper,
Dublin 1, DO1 C9W8, Ireland

First published in 2025

Text © 2025 Karen McCombie
Illustrations © 2025 Sofia Miller Salazar
Cover design © 2025 HarperCollins*Publishers* Limited

The moral right of Karen McCombie and Sofia Miller Salazar to be identified as the author and illustrator of this work has been asserted in accordance with the Copyright, Designs and Patents Act, 1988

ISBN 978-0-00-873673-6

10 9 8 7 6 5 4 3 2 1

All rights reserved. No part of this publication may be reproduced, stored in a retrieval system, or transmitted, in whole or in any part in any form or by any means, electronic, mechanical, photocopying, recording or otherwise without the prior permission in writing of the publisher and copyright owners

Without limiting the exclusive rights of any author, contributor or the publisher, any unauthorised use of this publication to train generative artificial intelligence (AI) technologies is expressly prohibited. HarperCollins also exercise their rights under Article 4(3) of the Digital Single Market Directive 2019/790 and expressly reserve this publication from the text and data mining exception

A catalogue record for this book is available from the British Library

Printed and bound in India by Replika Press Pvt. Ltd.

This book contains FSC™ certified paper and other controlled sources to ensure responsible forest management.

For more information visit: www.harpercollins.co.uk/green

*For Issy, my dancing buddy!*

# CONTENTS

## RUBY'S STORY

| | | |
|---|---|---|
| 1 | No More Exams | 3 |
| 2 | Too Many Surprises | 9 |
| 3 | Bumping into Max | 20 |
| 4 | Which Side Is Granny On? | 29 |
| 5 | Lucky at Last | 39 |

## YASMIN'S STORY

| | | |
|---|---|---|
| 6 | Pizza and Panic | 49 |
| 7 | The Worst Present | 55 |
| 8 | Never Alone | 62 |
| 9 | Secrets and Stress | 69 |
| 10 | Time for the Truth | 79 |

# RUBY'S STORY

# JUNE

## Chapter 1
## No More Exams

The final exam was over.

Ruby's very last GCSE exam.

She zoomed past the other students as they all came out of the school hall.

"Hey! No running!" a teacher yelled.

Ruby grinned and kept going. She burst into the playground and into the sunshine.

"Hey, Ruby-Roo!" someone shouted.

It was her best friend, Kam. His last exam was a few days ago, but he'd promised to meet Ruby when all her exams were finished too. They were going to get bubble tea and sit in the town square. Just to feel free. Free! No more schoolwork, no more nagging teachers. At least until the end of the summer.

Ruby waved to Kam. He was wearing his favourite cut-off denim shorts and a yellow crop top.

"Yay! Let's go have some fun, Roo!" Kam yelled.

"Don't call me that, Kam!" said Ruby. "Roo sounds like the name of a bunny on a kids' TV show!"

"But it's cute, like you!" said Kam. He grabbed Ruby and spun her around.

When he let go, Ruby looked back towards school. Her heart sank when she saw who was walking across the playground.

Her cousin Yasmin.

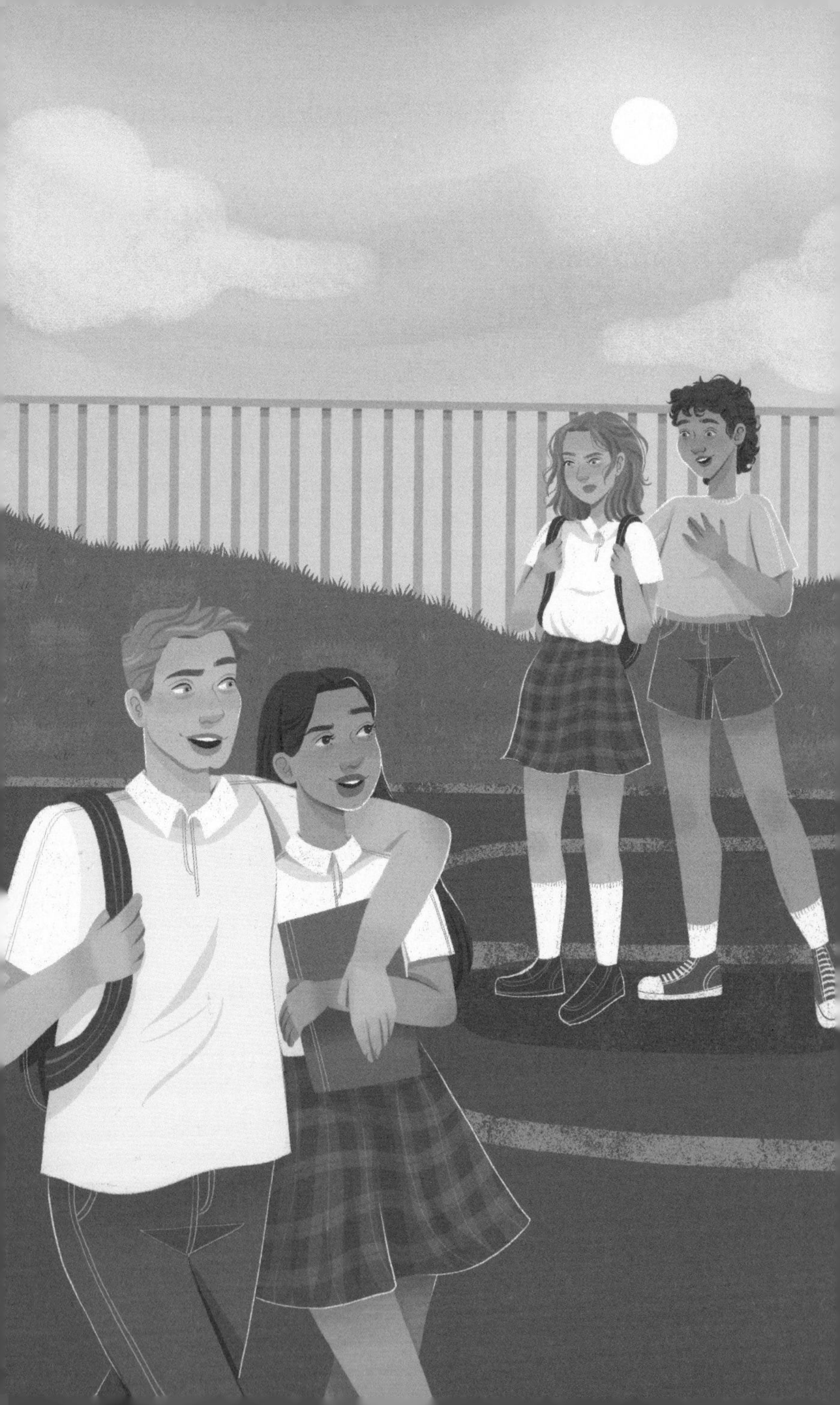

Yasmin's glossy hair hung down her back like brown satin. Her boyfriend Max had his arm around her.

"Wow, he is so lush ..." Kam sighed.

"What are you like?" Ruby laughed.

All Ruby wanted was to get away. Yasmin always made Ruby feel as if she was rubbish at everything.

Ruby wasn't sure she'd even pass today's exam. But whatever exam Yasmin had just finished she'd get top marks. Everything *always* went Yasmin's way.

When she was with her perfect cousin, Ruby felt small and hopeless.

And Ruby could tell that Yasmin got a kick out of that. In fact, Yasmin was staring over at Ruby right now and sneering ...

## Chapter 2
## Too Many Surprises

It was Granny's surprise birthday party that weekend. On Sunday afternoon, Ruby was in her aunt and uncle's garden, right at the back of a big crowd of people.

Granny stood under an arch of balloons with a big smile on her face while everyone sang "Happy Birthday".

Yasmin was with Uncle Carlo. Ruby took a quick photo of Yasmin's minidress. It was covered in shimmery blue sequins. Kam had to see this!

*OMG it's our gran's 65th birthday party, and Yasmin's dressed for a Taylor Swift concert!* Ruby messaged Kam.

A second later, her phone buzzed with Kam's reply.

*Can I borrow that dress for Pride next month?* he wrote, with a bunch of laugh emojis.

The Pride parade was happening in the city, a short train ride away. Ruby was going with him. Kam hadn't come out to his family yet, so the plan was that he'd wear his normal clothes to the station, then get changed in the train toilet.

"Thanks for this lovely surprise!" Ruby heard Granny call out, and everyone clapped.

"Hold it, folks!" Uncle Carlo shouted. "Sorry to hijack the party, but I've got another surprise – for my wonderful daughter!"

Everyone turned to look at Yasmin.

Uncle Carlo went on talking. "My darling, your mum and I are SO proud of you for working so hard for your exams!" said Uncle Carlo. "It's A-levels next, then you'll be off to university. Once you're a doctor, you'll be looking after us all!"

Granny's friends laughed, but Ruby felt sick. Sick of being the second-best cousin. Gutted that her own dad wasn't here. She'd never get to hear him make a speech like this ...

"Dad! Stop it!" Yasmin acted shy. Ruby knew it was fake. Her cousin loved all the attention.

"So here's a 'well done' present, darling," Uncle Carlo carried on. "It will help you get to your summer job ..."

Yasmin was going to tutor kids in Maths. Ruby's holiday job was working in a bakery.

There were oohs and ahhs from the crowd. Yasmin's boyfriend Max came round the side of the house pushing a brand-new bike. It had a big red bow on the handlebars.

He stopped near Ruby.

"Get on it, Yasmin!" said Uncle Carlo. "Give it a spin round the garden!"

Yasmin shook her head and didn't move. Uncle Carlo carried on making a big fuss of her. Auntie Jill joined in. While that was going on, Ruby looked at Max.

"Nice bike," she said.

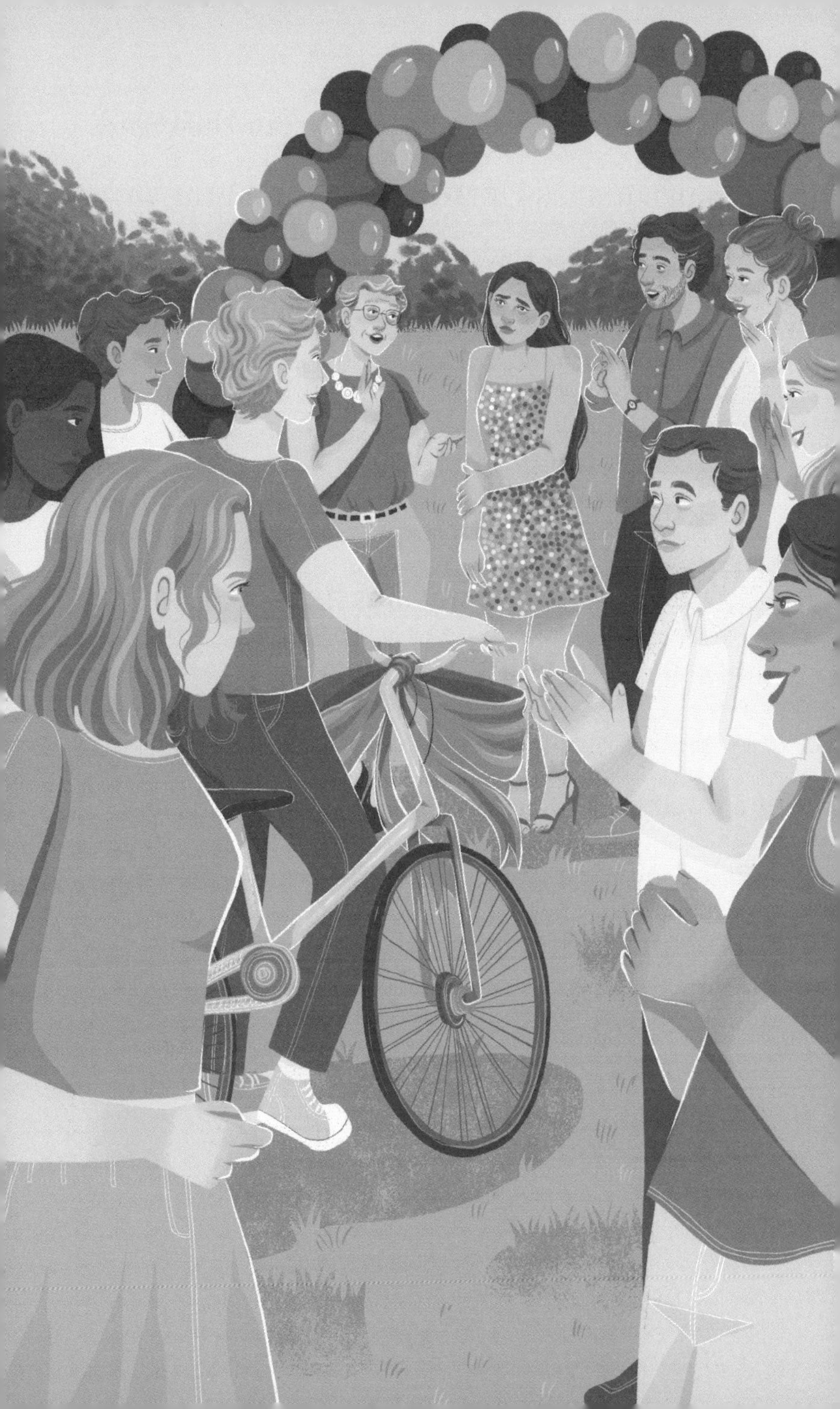

She'd never talked to him before. They'd never been in the same classes. He was even more cute close up. Kam would be jealous!

"It's the same make as my bike," said Max. "So it was my idea."

Ruby knew that her aunt and uncle really liked Yasmin's boyfriend. Auntie Jill was always going on about how great Max was. She'd told Ruby and her mum how Max wanted to be a sports coach. He and Yasmin planned to go to the same university.

Ruby wished she knew what her plans for the future were too ...

And then all of a sudden she heard someone shout.

She and Max turned – and saw Yasmin slump to the ground.

"Yasmin!" yelled Max. He shoved the bike at Ruby and ran to his girlfriend.

Ruby stared, then she remembered something.

This wasn't the first time Yasmin had fainted. It had happened plenty of times before. Like when they were little and Ruby got picked for the solo in their ballet show. And again when Ruby came first in the diving competition at the local pool.

Ruby wondered what had made Yasmin faint just now.

Hold on ...

Had Yasmin spotted Ruby talking to Max?

Was she jealous?

Was this what the drama was about?

# JULY

## Chapter 3
## Bumping into Max

The lido was crazy busy.

Small children were splashing and screeching in the pool.

"Why did I let you drag me here, Roo?" said Kam.

"Cos you want to get fit," Ruby reminded him. "And you hate the gym."

Kam didn't go to the gym cos his brother Alek worked there. Alek had muscles on his muscles. Kam's dad and Alek loved teasing Kam about how skinny he was.

"Come on then ..." Kam muttered.

But as soon as they both slipped into the water, Kam cheered up.

"Hey, isn't that Max?" he said, pointing at the far end of the pool.

"Oh, yeah!" said Ruby. Max had a T-shirt with *LIFEGUARD* on the front.

"Did you know he worked here, Roo?" Kam asked.

"No!" said Ruby. "Yasmin and me don't exactly talk much, do we?"

Kam grinned and said, "Well, let's show off our swimming skills then!"

*

Two hours later, the pool was emptying. Families were leaving with tired kids. Kam had left too. He'd got bored and he wanted to get to the shops before they shut. He still hadn't chosen what to wear for Pride next week.

Ruby stayed. She'd been working in the hot bakery all morning and it was bliss to be in the cool water.

She swam up to the edge of the pool and saw Max looking down at her.

"You're a pretty good swimmer, Roo!" he said.

"I used to be in the swim team when I was younger," Ruby replied. She pushed her wet hair off her face.

"Yeah?" said Max. "Why didn't you keep it up?"

"My mum couldn't afford all the trips to the swim meets," Ruby explained. "Not after my dad ..."

She stopped. The word was too hard to say.

"Sorry, Roo, I didn't mean to upset you!" Max said quickly.

"It's OK," said Ruby. "I just don't like to talk about it."

Max nodded. He looked as if he was about to leave. She didn't want him to.

"How's Yasmin getting on with her bike?" Ruby asked.

Max rolled his eyes. "Turns out it's broken. It's got to get fixed."

"But it's brand new!" said Ruby. "Still … Yasmin's never been into sporty stuff."

Max grinned. "No, she isn't. But I'll get her into it. What about you, Roo? Do you like sports?"

"I watch a lot on TV," said Ruby. "But hey, Max ... can you call me Ruby? I don't really like Roo."

"Sure!" he said. "But how come everyone calls you that?"

"Well, when I started secondary school, I said my name was Ruby," she began. "But then Yasmin told everyone to call me Roo. It stuck after that."

"That sucks!" said Max.

Ruby nodded.

"You and Yasmin don't really get on, do you?" said Max.

"We're just different, I suppose," Ruby said. She couldn't tell Max how Yasmin made her feel.

"Hey, listen, Ruby, there's a sponsored swim at the lido soon. To raise money for the food bank. Why don't you join in?"

Ruby liked that Max had used her full name.

"Um, maybe," she said. "I'd just need to get a lot fitter!"

"You look pretty fit already," said Max with a cheeky grin.

Ruby felt herself blush.

She pushed off backwards, letting the water cool her hot cheeks ...

## Chapter 4
## Which Side Is Granny On?

It was Saturday, and Ruby had just finished her shift at the bakery. She'd come round to Granny's with her sponsor form.

"You're raising money for the food bank? That's a good cause!" said Granny as she picked up her pen. "What about asking your auntie

Jill and uncle Carlo? I'm sure they'd love to support you!"

"I don't mean to sound funny, Granny, but I don't want them to know," Ruby told her. "They might think Yasmin should do the swim too. And I just want it to be *my* thing."

Granny frowned. "But didn't Yasmin's boyfriend tell you about the swim? Won't he tell Yasmin anyway?" she said.

"I asked Max not to. I said it was going to be a surprise for my family," said Ruby.

Max keeping Ruby's secret – it felt good.

"I see," said Granny. "It makes me sad that you girls don't get on any more. When you were little, you always played together."

Ruby gave a shrug. Yasmin was all smiles around Granny. How could Ruby explain what her cousin was really like?

"Listen, Ruby," said Granny softly. "I know it was awful what happened with your dad and everything ..."

*Everything.*

Granny was talking about Mum and Ruby suddenly being poor. And how they had to move from their nice house to the tiny flat above the supermarket.

"It must be hard for you when you look at all the stuff that Yasmin gets; I know things aren't so easy for you and your mum. But, Ruby, it's not Yasmin's fault that—"

Ruby felt a punch of hurt and anger.

Granny thought she was jealous of Yasmin? *Really?!?*

"You have no idea, Granny!" Ruby burst out. "Yasmin's *always* trying to put me down. She's been like that all our lives! Even before Dad ..."

She couldn't go on. It hurt too much.

Ruby snatched up the sponsor sheet and stormed off.

"Ruby! Don't go!" Granny called after her.

But Ruby slammed the front door and sped off towards the lido. On the way, she felt her bag vibrate. She'd shoved her mobile in there this morning before her shift.

Maybe it was a text from Granny, saying sorry.

Instead, it was a message from Kam. The first of LOADS of missed calls and messages from Kam!

"Oh no," Ruby muttered as she read the messages.

*Where are you? The train will be here in 5 mins!*

*ROO! I am starting to panic! I need you and I need my bag!*

*Look, I'm on the train. Please call me! Meet at Pride! PLEASE bring my clothes!*

Ruby felt terrible. She'd been so busy with work and training for the fundraiser that she'd forgotten what day it was. The day of the Pride parade. Kam's special day! She looked at her watch. She'd never make it now.

*SO SO SORRY!* she messaged Kam. *Family stuff. I'll explain later. X*

Kam would have fun without her, she was sure. But she felt bad about his new clothes for Pride. He'd stashed them at her house. His brother must never know about them, or about Kam going on the Pride parade.

"Hi, Ruby!"

It was Max. He had a takeaway in his hands.

"Late lunch!" he said with a smile. "Want a chip?"

Ruby smiled back, then a loud ping of a message on her phone made her jump. It was Kam.

*OK. But are you still coming, Roo? Are you on the next train?*

How was Ruby ever going to break the bad news to Kam? No way did she have time to meet him at the Pride parade.

Then Kam pinged again. With a photo this time.

*The parade's just about to start, but look who I just spotted!*

The photo was of Yasmin. She was standing in a doorway with some young guy. They were looking into each other's eyes!

"What's up?" Max asked. "Wait, is that Yasmin?"

Ruby gasped as Max grabbed her phone and zoomed in on his girlfriend and whoever she was with ...

# AUGUST

## Chapter 5
## Lucky at Last

Today was exam results day.

Ruby's head spun with worry as she walked to school.

Would her grades be good enough to get into sixth form?

What if she ran into Kam? They had fallen out badly and hadn't spoken in weeks. He'd totally flipped out at her when she didn't make it to Pride.

And would Yasmin be showing off about her top marks as always?

"Hey, Ruby!" she heard Max call out as she got to the school gate.

They were getting pretty friendly. Ruby had started going to the lido most days to train for the sponsored swim, and Max always chatted to her when he was on his break. Sometimes it felt kind of flirty, but Ruby knew that couldn't be true. He was with Yasmin. Perfect Yasmin.

"Hi, Max!" she said. "Yasmin not with you?"

"Nah, she told me she'd see me here," Max replied.

Things seemed to have cooled between Max and Yasmin since the day of the Pride parade. Max had been right beside her when Ruby was sent the photo from Kam – the picture of Yasmin talking to another guy. Max had called Yasmin right away. He had to know what she was up to. But she didn't answer – it went to voicemail.

Next day at the lido, Max told Ruby what Yasmin had said about the guy in the photo. She'd said Granny had bought something online from the guy and Yasmin had gone to the city to collect it. Was that true? Did Max believe it? Ruby wasn't so sure.

She had planned to ask Granny about it, to see if it was a lie or not. But then Granny always backed Yasmin, so Ruby didn't bother.

"Wow, it's so busy!" said Ruby as she and Max walked into the crowded school hall.

"Here!" said a teacher, passing Max and Ruby's results to them.

Max looked at his first.

"Yes! All good!" said Max, punching the air. "What about you, Ruby?"

Ruby blinked. "My marks are OK!" she gasped. "It means I've got my place in sixth form!"

"We'll be there together," said Max softly.

Ruby took a short, sharp breath.

What did Max mean? He sounded like he wanted her to be his girlfriend. That couldn't be true, surely?

But Max meant what he said – just the way it sounded.

Cos then he leaned forward and kissed her.

It only lasted a second, but it was everything.

"Sorry ... I've really wanted to do that for a while now," said Max.

At that moment, Ruby spotted her cousin. She was at the far side of the hall. Yasmin stared at Ruby.

Ruby turned back to Max.

She smiled and said, "Me too."

This perfect moment wasn't Yasmin's for once. It was Ruby's.

And Ruby kissed Max right back ...

# YASMIN'S STORY

# JUNE

## Chapter 6
## Pizza and Panic

The final exam was over!

There was a crush of students leaving the school hall. Yasmin's heart beat fast. Way too fast.

She had to get some air ...

Then just as she stepped outside, an arm came around her neck. She was trapped in a headlock.

"Hey, Yasmin! Wait for me!" said Max.

He pulled her close and kissed the top of her head.

Yasmin gulped for air. It wasn't just cos of the way Max was holding her. It was also cos of what she'd done in the exam ...

"Ready for Pizza Zone?" asked Max.

Yasmin really didn't want to go to the Pizza Zone cafe. It was always full and noisy.

"Can't we just get some picnic things and sit in the park?" she asked.

"Picnics are for kids!" Max laughed.

Yasmin smiled and nodded. After four months of going out together, she knew Max would always just grin and get his way.

"Come on – it'll be fun," said Max. His arm hugged her extra hard.

Yasmin bit her lip.

It was all feeling too much, too hard. All the exams, her parents' plans for her, plans for the future ...

And now she looked up and saw that someone was watching her.

It was her cousin Ruby, standing by the school gates with her cute friend Kam.

There was nothing cute about Ruby.

Her cousin's eyes felt like laser beams. It had been like this since they were kids. Even back then, Ruby would glare at Yasmin like she hated her.

Suddenly, Yasmin felt as if all the panic was going to drag her down and make her pass out.

*"Take slow breaths and tell yourself it will pass ..."*

That was Granny's advice for Yasmin about the panic attacks.

"It will pass, it will pass, it will pass ..." Yasmin said silently to herself.

At the same time, she tried to smile at her cousin.

Ruby turned away.

## Chapter 7
## The Worst Present

That weekend, Mum and Auntie Suzie were fussing with Granny's birthday cake.

Yasmin looked around, but the garden was so crowded that she couldn't see Ruby.

"You look amazing!" Dad said to her.

Yasmin didn't feel amazing. She felt like a Christmas bauble in the shiny dress her mum had made her wear.

*"Happy birthday to you ...!"* people began to sing.

Yasmin tried to smile and join in.

Then she spotted Ruby over by the house. Ruby held up her mobile. Was her cousin taking a photo of Granny? No. The phone was pointing at Yasmin.

Was Ruby planning to stick the photo on some Snapchat group and make fun of Yasmin? It had happened before. Last year,

Yasmin's friends Fran and Eleni showed her a bitchy post online. It was a photo of Yasmin in a swimsuit, aged ten, mucking around and posing in a paddling pool in Ruby's garden.

*Guess the show-off!* it said on the post.

Yasmin told her mum, but Ruby deleted the post. Mum said Yasmin should give Ruby a break after what had happened with Ruby's dad. So Yasmin decided not to moan about Ruby ever again.

Only Granny knew. And Fran and Eleni. Though she hadn't seen much of the girls since she'd got together with Max. He took up all of her time.

Yasmin snapped out of that memory when she heard what her dad was saying ...

"Sorry to hijack the party, but I've got another surprise – for my wonderful daughter!"

Yasmin froze as her dad gave some gushy speech about her.

Her parents were always doing this. Making her sound like she was so special. And when they did it in front of Ruby, it made everything a hundred times worse between the cousins. When Yasmin had said so to Mum and Dad, they'd told her she was being silly.

Just like they told her she was being silly when she tried to say that she didn't want to be a doctor ...

All of a sudden, everyone was looking towards the side of the house. There was Max, holding a bike with a big red bow on it.

The panic began inside her.

Yasmin didn't want this present. She didn't like cycling. She felt wobbly and scared on roads.

But it wasn't just the bike that was making Yasmin panic. The stress of letting her parents down was too much. Like the time she lost the solo at ballet to Ruby or when Ruby won the diving competition. She'd seen the way Mum and Dad had looked at her, so sad.

And they were going to kill Yasmin when they found out her secret about the exams ...

This time the panic came too quickly for her to do anything.

Yasmin blacked out.

# JULY

## Chapter 8
## Never Alone

The sun was warm on Yasmin's face. The music in her headphones was pumping. Both things made her feel better. She'd been teaching Maths to bored kids all day. She felt really tired.

It didn't matter how good the pay was, Yasmin didn't like her summer job. She didn't blame the kids. Who wanted to do lessons in the holidays? She bet they'd much rather hang out in the park with their friends.

The park ... that sounded nice. Yasmin was meeting Max at the lido, but that wasn't for a while.

Five minutes later, she was strolling in the park with an ice cream. Yasmin watched people on pedalos on the lake. She had done that last summer with Fran and Eleni. It was such a laugh! She should hang out with them again soon. But Max didn't really like the girls for some reason.

Yasmin nearly dropped the ice cream as her phone buzzed.

"Hey, hi!" she said cheerfully as Max's face filled the screen.

He looked cross.

"What are you doing in the park?" he asked.

Yasmin shivered, even in the sunshine.

She hated the Together24/7 app Max had put on her phone. He said it would be good cos they'd always know where the other was. But it made her feel like she couldn't breathe.

"I had a bit of extra time," she said.

"Well, I'm ready *now*, and you're still ten minutes away!" said Max. "If your bike wasn't broken, you'd be here sooner."

Yasmin almost smiled. The back wheel was bent as if someone had kicked it. To be honest, Yasmin wondered if Ruby had done it at Granny's party. If she had, Ruby had done Yasmin a favour! It meant she didn't have to ride the stupid thing.

"Hey, guess who showed up at the lido today?" Max said now.

"Who?" asked Yasmin as she tried to walk faster.

"Your cousin," said Max.

"Oh, OK," said Yasmin. "So did you talk to Roo?"

Yasmin was puzzled. What had made Ruby go swimming? She'd given it up years ago, saying it was boring and only for nerds (Yasmin was still in the swim team back then).

Then Yasmin remembered her mum boasting to Auntie Suzie and Ruby about what a nice boy Max was. How he'd got a job as a lifeguard over summer. Ruby knew he'd be at the lido! What was she doing there too?

What was Ruby playing at?

"Actually, she asked me to call her Ruby," said Max. "She told me that you got everyone at school to call her Roo and she hates it."

"No, I didn't!" said Yasmin. "She loved that name! It was what her dad called her!"

"Didn't sound like that to me," Max said.

Yasmin said nothing.

Why did Ruby have to blame her for everything?

# Chapter 9
# Secrets and Stress

Granny and Yasmin had their secrets.

Their secret chats about how low Yasmin was feeling.

It was why Granny had booked her a counselling session in the city.

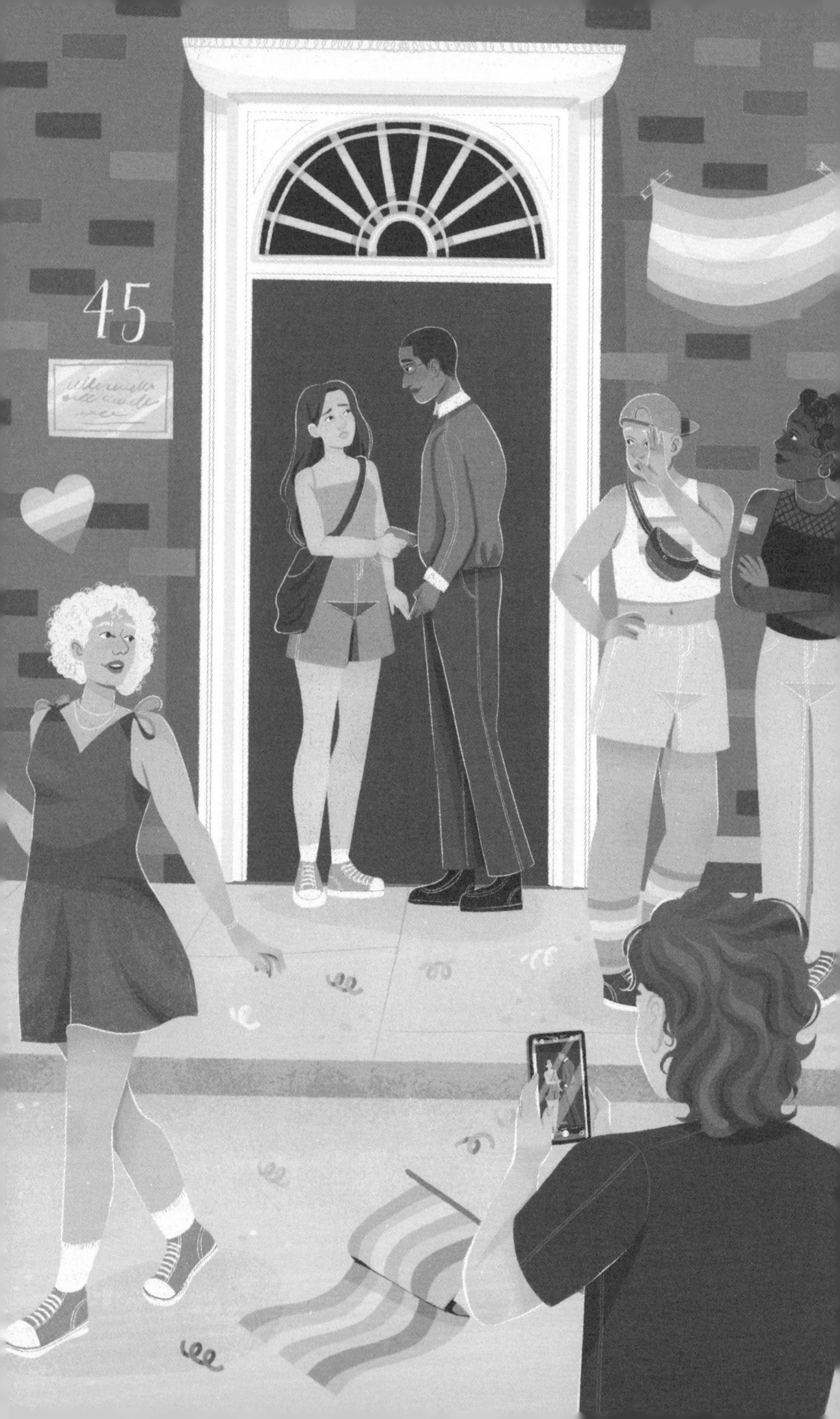
45

Granny felt bad not telling Yasmin's parents, but then Yasmin's parents were the ones stressing her out.

It had been good to see that the counsellor Tariq was quite young. It made Yasmin feel less nervy. It had taken her a while to start talking, but then the hour had whizzed by.

When she came out of Tariq's office, the Pride parade was over. The road was still covered in confetti as Yasmin ran for her train.

She got to the train just in time and flopped down on an empty seat.

"Oh, hi!" said the boy in the next seat. It was Ruby's friend Kam.

"Uh, hi!" said Yasmin.

"Hey, I saw you earlier," Kam said. "With a guy."

Yasmin felt sick.

"Um ... my gran ordered something on eBay. It was from that guy. I was picking it up for her," she lied. "So were you here for Pride today?"

Yasmin was sure Kam was gay, but he was wearing a black T-shirt and combat trousers. Not exactly a Pride look!

Also, Kam seemed kind of down.

"I tagged along at the edge of the parade," Kam told her. "But it all felt wrong. I had these rainbow dungarees and a purple feather boa, but they were at Ruby's house. She said she was going to come with me, but then she forgot about Pride. Well, so she *said* ..."

That last comment sounded kind of bitchy.

"What do you mean?" Yasmin asked Kam. But she felt a chill. She always felt a chill when it came to Ruby.

"Sorry, Yasmin, but I think she fancies your boyfriend!" Kam burst out. "She's been obsessed with going to the lido cos he's there. She'd rather do that than come with me to Pride!"

Yasmin said nothing. But it made total sense.

"When she told me she wasn't coming, I got mad and I said all that to her," Kam went on. "I don't think we're talking now."

"She'll come round," said Yasmin. She didn't really believe that. Ruby was great at being mad at people, as Yasmin knew.

"I don't think so. She left a message saying I was a terrible friend cos I'd forgotten it's nearly the anniversary of her losing her dad."

Yasmin frowned. "Hold on," she said. "You don't think Ruby's dad is dead, do you?"

"Huh? Well, yeah! Isn't he?" Kam looked shocked.

"No! He left her and her mum for another woman. He ran off with all their money," Yasmin told him.

It was a wicked thing for her uncle to have done. But it was wicked for Ruby to let her best friend think her dad was dead. Was she making other people think that too? So that people would feel sorry for her?

Before Kam could say anything else, his phone buzzed.

While he checked his message, Yasmin pulled out her mobile. She'd turned it off while she was in the city.

Just as she switched it back on, Kam screamed a loud "No, no, NO!!"

"What's wrong?" Yasmin asked.

Kam was shaking.

"It's my brother Alek! What has she done? WHAT HAS RUBY DONE TO ME?" Kam shouted.

Yasmin looked at the message on his screen.

*So your little friend dropped your backpack off at the gym,* it said. *The zip was open. I saw what was inside. Wait till I tell Dad, you little—*

The word that came next was horrible. Yasmin gasped. And then she jumped as her phone buzzed too.

It was a voicemail from Max, sent an hour ago.

*What are you doing in the city?* Max demanded. *Who's the guy in the photo I just saw? The one Ruby's mate took?*

Yasmin felt the panic grab hold again. Tariq the counsellor had helped her look at why her parents made her feel stressed. But they hadn't even started on the stress caused by Ruby.

Or by Max ...

# AUGUST

## Chapter 10
## Time For the Truth

No one else's parents were here.

Yasmin was the only one whose mum and dad were in the school hall with her while she collected her results.

It was so embarrassing ...

And now she was even more embarrassed cos Mum was crying and Dad was hitting the roof.

"There's been a mistake. These results can't be Yasmin's!" Dad shouted at Mr Marlow, the headteacher.

Yasmin knew there was no mistake. This was her secret plan. She'd made sure she failed her science exams. It meant she'd never be able to study to be a doctor. She just didn't know how to explain why she'd done it to her parents.

And then she froze.

Ruby and Max were on the other side of the crowded hall.

Max was *kissing* Ruby.

Then Ruby stared right over at Yasmin.

Yasmin watched as her cousin put her arms around Max's neck and kissed him back.

In that second, Yasmin knew Ruby wanted to hurt her. Ruby must think that she'd won.

But instead, with that kiss, Ruby had set Yasmin free.

Yasmin was done with Max bossing her around, telling her where they were going to eat, who she could be friends with, what university they were both going to go to.

She didn't want him spying on where she was all the time.

She didn't want his arm around her neck ever again.

Ruby was welcome to him!

All of a sudden, *everything* felt easier …

"Mum, Dad, Mr Marlow," Yasmin began, "I'm not going to sixth form. I'm going to college in the city. I've been offered a place on an Events Management course."

It was Yasmin's dream career. She loved music. She wanted to work with bands and organise concerts and travel the world.

"What? What even *is* that?" Yasmin's mum sounded horrified.

Yasmin ignored her. She also ignored Dad and Mr Marlow, who were talking too fast at her.

Yasmin had something important to do.

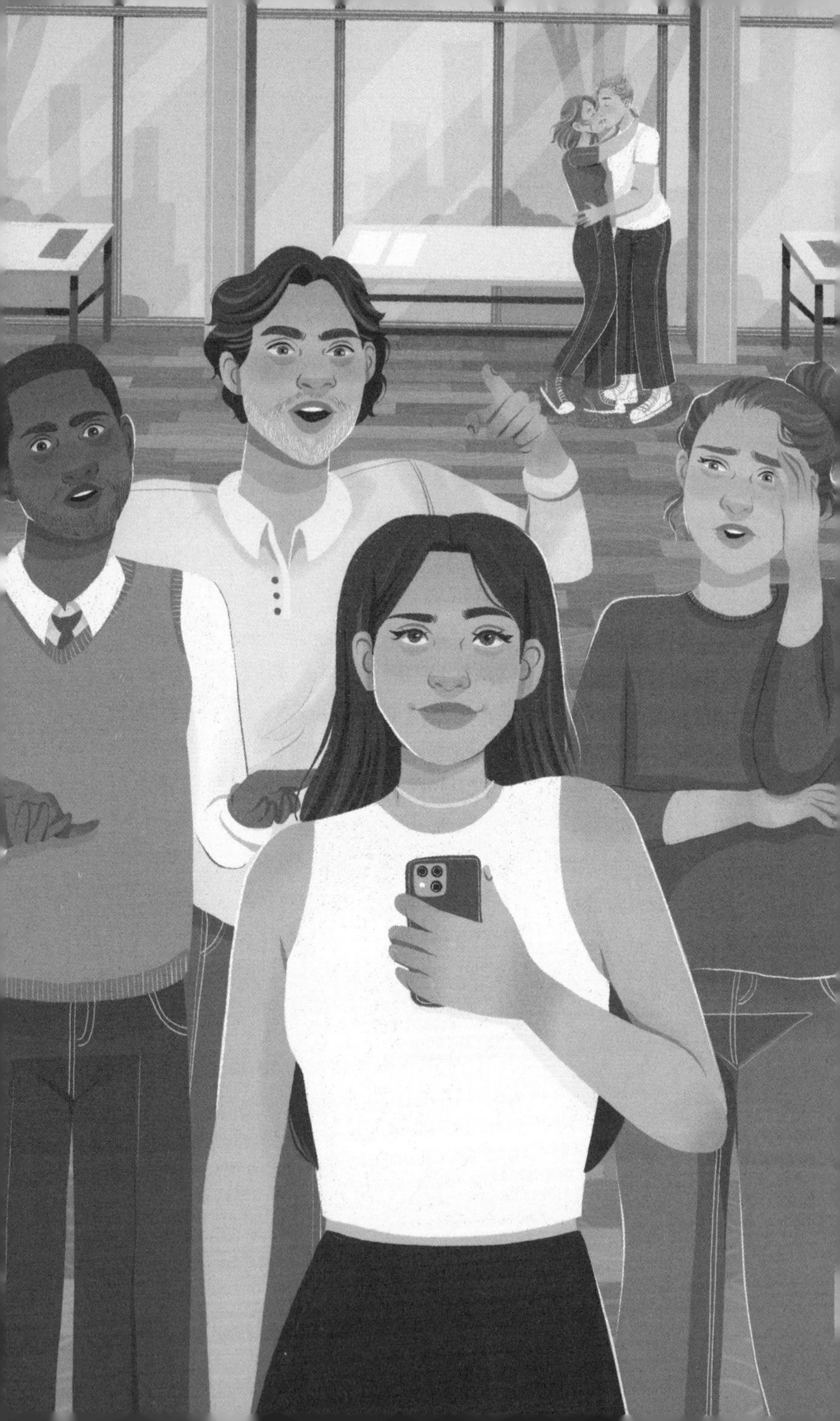

She took her phone from her pocket and deleted Max's number. She deleted the Together24/7 app.

Max, her parents and especially her cousin Ruby – she wouldn't let any of them upset her again.

She was going to be her own person.

Yasmin smiled as everyone around her freaked out.

Our books are tested
for children and young people by
children and young people.

Thanks to everyone who consulted on
a manuscript for their time and effort in
helping us to make our books better
for our readers.